THE NHL: HISTORY AND HEROES

MONTREAL CANADIENS

MICHAEL E. GOODMAN

THE NHL: HISTORY AND HEROES

Published by Creative Education
P.O. Box 227, Mankato, Minnesota 56002
Creative Education is an imprint of The Creative Company.

DESIGN AND PRODUCTION BY **ZENO DESIGN**

Printed in the United States of America

PHOTOGRAPHS BY Corbis (Bettmann, Reuters), Getty Images (Allsport/Allsport, Brian Babineau/NHLI, Denis Brodeur/NHLI, Bruce Bennett Studios, Kevin C. Cox, Charles Laberge, Andre Pichette, Andre Ringuette/NHLI, Dave Sanford, George Silk//Time Life Pictures, Yves Marcoux, Pictorial Parade, Dave Sanford/NHLI), Hockey Hall of Fame (Imperial Oil-Turofsky)

LIBRARY OF CONGRESS CATALOGING-IN-PUBLICATION DATA

Goodman, Michael E.
The story of the Montreal Canadiens / by Michael E. Goodman.
p. cm. — (The NHL: history and heroes)
Includes index
ISBN 978-1-58341-618-1
1. Montreal Canadiens (Hockey team)—History—Juvenile literature. I. Title.

GV848.M6G665 2008
796.962'640971428—dc22 2007018962

First Edition

9 8 7 6 5 4 3 2 1

COVER: Goaltender Cristobal Huet

CREATIVE EDUCATION

MONTREAL CANADIENS

MONTREAL

IT'S MAY 24, 1986, AND THE MONTREAL CANADIENS ARE SET TO BECOME THE MOST SUCCESSFUL NORTH AMERICAN PROFESSIONAL SPORTS FRANCHISE OF ALL TIME. A WIN TONIGHT IN CALGARY, ALBERTA, WILL GIVE THE CANADIENS THEIR 23RD STANLEY CUP AS CHAMPIONS OF THE NATIONAL HOCKEY LEAGUE, PUTTING THEM PAST THE NEW YORK YANKEES, WHO HAVE WON 22 WORLD TITLES IN MAJOR LEAGUE BASEBALL. LED BY 20-YEAR-OLD ROOKIE GOALTENDER PATRICK ROY (*RUH-WAH*), THE CANADIENS, UP THREE GAMES TO ONE IN THE STANLEY CUP FINALS, ARE

CANADIENS

DOMINATING THE CALGARY FLAMES IN GAME 5. THEN, IN THE CLOSING MINUTES, THE FLAMES RALLY. THEY SCORE TWICE TO MAKE THE SCORE 4–3 AND CONTINUE ATTACKING THE MONTREAL NET FOR THE TYING GOAL. WITH JUST 14 SECONDS LEFT, CALGARY DEFENDER JAMIE MACOUN SEES AN OPENING AND FIRES OFF A POINT-BLANK SLAP SHOT. INSTINCTIVELY, ROY DIVES AND SLAPS THE PUCK ASIDE WITH HIS STICK, PRESERVING THE VICTORY AND ASSURING CHAMPIONSHIP NUMBER 23 FOR THE CANADIENS.

WINNING IN TWO LANGUAGES

IN 1535, FRENCH EXPLORER JACQUES CARTIER sailed down the Saint Lawrence River in Eastern Canada to an island that featured a three-peaked mountain he called *Montreal*, or "Mount Royal." More than 100 years later, French fur traders established a town on the island, and colonists began crossing the Atlantic to settle there. These colonists were sometimes called *les habitants*, French for "the inhabitants." Even when the city came under British control in 1760, most Montreal residents continued to speak French.

By the early 1900s, hockey had become the most popular sport in Montreal and the rest of Canada, no matter which language players and fans spoke. At the time, most of Montreal's professional teams represented the city's English-speaking community, and French citizens clamored for their own team.

The second-largest city in Canada and the fourth-largest French-speaking city in the world, Montreal has a rich sports and cultural history.

That franchise, called the Club de Hockey Canadien, was finally formed in December 1909. Although officially known as the Canadiens, the team was nicknamed "Les Habitants," or "Habs" for short.

The Canadiens played their first games on an outdoor rink called the Jubilee, often in below-zero temperatures. For the team's first game on January 5, 1910, more than 3,000 enthusiastic fans braved the bitter cold and were rewarded with a 7–6 overtime victory. The club's offense was led in those early years by defenseman Jack Laviolette and center Edouard "Newsy" Lalonde, and the nets were guarded by legendary goaltender Georges Vezina, one of hockey's most dominant players. Vezina starred for more than 15 seasons in Montreal and was later inducted as one of the charter members of the Hockey Hall of Fame. In his memory, the National Hockey League (NHL) honors the best goaltender each year with the Vezina Trophy. The all-French club had

CANADIENS ALL-TIME TEAM

Jean Béliveau CENTER

It was fitting that Jean Béliveau played center on the ice because, for 20 seasons, he was the heart of the Canadiens. He played on 10 Stanley Cup winners for the Habs and captained five of those teams. Big and powerful, Béliveau was outstanding on the ice and outspoken in politics as well. When many French-speaking citizens in Quebec wanted their province to separate from Canada, Béliveau urged them to stay in the union while still preserving their French heritage. His words helped reduce calls for secession. "Béliveau provides hockey with a magnificent image—a true role model," said NHL president Clarence Campbell.

CANADIENS SEASONS: 1950–71
HEIGHT: 6-3 (190.5 cm)
WEIGHT: 205 (93 kg)

- 507 career goals
- 712 career assists
- 13-time All-Star
- Hockey Hall of Fame inductee (1972)

This display honors the 1915–16 Canadiens—led by such greats as Newsy Lalonde and Georges Vezina—who won the franchise's first Stanley Cup.

some early success, but the team really began to excel once it permitted top English-speaking players to join in 1915.

The next season, the bilingual Canadiens won the National Hockey Association title (the NHL was not formed until 1917) with a 16–7–1 record and defeated the Portland Rosebuds of the Pacific Coast Hockey Association in a special playoff to win their first Stanley Cup—the big silver chalice awarded to the world champion. Each Canadiens player received $238 as victory pay.

The Canadiens did not win a second Cup until eight years later, in 1924. By that time, the club was led by its first scoring star, Howarth "Howie" Morenz from Stratford, Ontario. Morenz, who was known as the "Stratford Streak," had blazing speed and a powerful shot. "His speed was incredible," said Toronto Maple Leafs defenseman King Clancy. "I remember him coming down the ice right at me one game. My defense partner and I pulled together and thought we had him stopped. But he never broke stride. He slid the puck between us and leaped about three feet off the ice, picked up the puck, and scored."

In Montreal's 1923 training camp, Morenz won a spot at center between high-scoring wings Aurel Joliat and Billy Boucher. He scored a goal in his NHL debut in December 1923, and by the time the season was over, Morenz had propelled the Canadiens to their second Stanley Cup. But that was just the beginning. Morenz played 12 seasons in Montreal and ranked among the top 10 scorers in the NHL each year. He led the Habs to the Cup two more times (in 1930 and 1931) and earned three Hart Trophies as the NHL's Most Valuable Player (MVP). The Stratford Streak helped make the Canadiens' new home, an arena called the Montreal Forum, the center of the hockey world.

Honoring Georges

ON OPENING NIGHT IN NOVEMBER 1925, Georges Vezina was guarding the Montreal net for the 16th straight season. Vezina collapsed on the ice midway through the second period and had to be carried from the arena and hospitalized. Before the end of the season, he died of tuberculosis, a disease of the lungs. Despite suffering from the disease for more than three years, Vezina had consistently posted the best goals against average (GAA) in the league. Because he performed so well despite breathing and fatigue problems, most teammates and fans didn't realize how sick Vezina was. Following his death, the owners of the Canadiens donated a new trophy to the NHL to honor both his skill and courage. It would be given annually to the full-time goaltender who had allowed the fewest goals during the regular season. Fittingly, the first winner of the Vezina Trophy—awarded following the 1926–27 season—was George Hainsworth, who had replaced Vezina as the Canadiens' goalie. Since that time, 27 more Vezina Trophies have been awarded to Montreal goaltenders, the most of any team. The most recent Canadiens winner was José Théodore, who earned both the Vezina Trophy and league MVP award in 2001–02.

SOARING WITH THE ROCKET

THE GREAT DEPRESSION HURT CANADIAN hockey in the 1930s, especially in Montreal. The city's English-speaking NHL team, the Maroons, folded in 1938, while the Canadiens barely managed to survive financially. The Habs struggled in the league standings, too, falling into last place by 1939–40. Then they began a meteoric rise in the early 1940s, led by a high-flying winger from the tough Bordeaux section of Montreal named Maurice "Rocket" Richard.

Richard earned his nickname because of his high-speed manuevers on skates and supercharged slap shot. A scoring machine who would thrill Montreal fans for 18 seasons (1942–60), Richard was sometimes called the "Babe Ruth of hockey." Like the Babe, Richard was a flamboyant offensive standout

Among Maurice "Rocket" Richard's many memorable feats were three hat tricks (at least three goals per game) during the 1944 Stanley Cup Finals.

who helped turn his team into a dynasty. During Richard's years in Montreal, the Canadiens won eight regular-season championships (with the NHL's best record) and captured eight Stanley Cups, including five in a row from 1956 to 1960. When Babe Ruth hit 60 home runs during the 1927 season, he astounded the sports world. Richard's 50 goals in 50 games during the 1944–45 season was just as remarkable a feat. It would be 36 years before another NHL player (winger Mike Bossy of the New York Islanders) scored that many goals so quickly. In 1958, Richard became hockey's first 600-goal scorer (playoff goals included). And he had an unrivaled drive to win. A reporter once asked him which goals he remembered most vividly. "The only goals I remember are ones that win games for the Canadiens," Rocket replied.

Richard teamed with left wing Hector "Toe" Blake and center Elmer Lach to form the "Punch Line," the most potent scoring trio in the NHL in the 1940s.

CANADIENS ALL-TIME TEAM

Maurice Richard WING

Long before Wayne Gretzky came along, Maurice Richard was hockey's greatest scorer. "Rocket" showed his scoring talent early, tallying 32 goals in only 46 games during his first full season in the NHL (1943–44), then contributing 12 goals in 9 contests to lead Montreal to the Stanley Cup that postseason. Scoring goals was almost automatic for him. In one 1952 playoff game, Richard was knocked unconscious by a body check. He was revived but was only partially conscious when he scored the game-winning goal that night. In Richard's honor, the top goal scorer during the regular season each year is awarded the Maurice Richard Trophy.

CANADIENS SEASONS: 1942–60
HEIGHT: 5-10 (178 cm)
WEIGHT: 180 (82 kg)

- 82 career playoff goals
- 13-time All-Star
- 1947 Hart Trophy winner (as league MVP)
- Hockey Hall of Fame inductee (1961)

The famous "Punch Line" of Maurice Richard (left), Elmer Lach (middle), and Hector "Toe" Blake (right) dominated from 1943 to 1948.

But they were just three of the standouts on the Canadiens roster. The Habs also featured goaltender Bill Durnan and defenseman Emile "Butch" Bouchard. Together, they led the Canadiens to Stanley Cup wins in 1944 and 1946 and to the Cup Finals in 1947.

Although Richard set numerous scoring records during his career, he never won a season points (goals plus assists) scoring title. He came closest during the 1954–55 season. Richard was ahead in the scoring race with four games left when he got involved in a brawl and was suspended for the rest of the season. Fellow Canadiens wing Bernard "Boom Boom" Geoffrion ended up passing Richard in points. Montreal fans, angry with the suspension of their hero, rioted during the last game of the season, damaging the Forum and destroying much of downtown Montreal. Peace was restored only when Richard went on the radio and begged fans to stop the destruction.

Richard remained a folk hero in Canada even after he retired from hockey. When he died in May 2000 after a long battle with cancer, he was given a state funeral broadcast on television and radio across the country—the first time a Canadian athlete had ever been given such an honor.

"Stressful? How would you like a job where, every time you make a mistake, a big red light goes on and 18,000 people boo?"

MONTREAL GOALTENDER JACQUES PLANTE

The Richard Riot

MAURICE "ROCKET" RICHARD WAS USED to being checked hard by opposing players, but he was also ready to fight back. In a game near the end of the 1954–55 season, Boston Bruins defenseman Hal Laycoe hit Richard with a high stick, cutting his head. Richard used his own stick to retaliate against Laycoe and then smacked a linesman who came between the players. As a result, NHL president Clarence Campbell suspended Richard for the rest of the season and the playoffs, angering Montreal fans. Campbell insisted on attending the final Canadiens home game, against the wishes of the city's mayor. Midway through the game, fans began pelting Campbell with vegetables and eggs they had brought to the Forum for that purpose, and someone even set off a tear gas bomb. Officials stopped the game, declaring a forfeit. As fans poured outside, they began vandalizing local stores, and more than 60 people were arrested. Richard, watching the game from the stands, took the radio microphone to calm fans. "I will take my punishment and come back next year to help the club and the young players win the Cup," Richard promised. He lived up to his word; 12 months later, the Habs were champs again.

THE MONTREAL MONOPOLY

THINGS WERE PEACEFUL OUTSIDE THE FORUM as the 1955–56 season opened, but the excitement inside the building was just starting. The Habs were about to begin one of the most remarkable runs in NHL history. New coach Toe Blake had assembled a star-studded lineup that included wingers Richard, Geoffrion, and Dickie Moore; Rocket's brother Henri Richard and fellow center Jean Béliveau; defensemen Doug Harvey and Tom Johnson; and goalie Jacques Plante. All of these players were future Hall-of-Famers.

This powerful Canadiens team won five straight Stanley Cups from 1956 to 1960, when the Rocket retired. Then, led by the 6-foot-3 (190.5 cm) Béliveau, the Habs captured five more Cups in the seven seasons between 1965 and 1971. Montreal was so dominant that it caused the NHL to make a rule change. Prior to the 1960s, players

One of the classiest—and most successful—players in NHL history, center Jean Béliveau helped the Canadiens capture the Stanley Cup 10 times.

assessed a minor penalty had to sit out a full two minutes in the penalty box. The Canadiens' power play was so effective, however, that Montreal could routinely score two or three goals during a two-minute penalty and put the game out of reach. To keep games closer and more competitive, the NHL decided that a player serving a minor penalty could return to the game if a goal was scored against his team—a rule that still stands today.

> **"I want to be humble, but our record [of five consecutive Stanley Cups in the 1950s] will never be beaten.... As far as I'm concerned, we had the best team ever in the National Hockey League."**
>
> MONTREAL WING BERNARD "BOOM BOOM" GEOFFRION

Throughout these glory years, Béliveau served as the team's captain and offensive leader. He was the first recipient of the Conn Smythe Trophy as playoff MVP when the Canadiens won the 1965 Cup, and in his final season, 1971, he led Montreal to another championship by scoring 22 points in 20 playoff games. But just as important as Béliveau's scoring ability was his unselfish passing ability, which helped turn several talented young wings—such as Gilles Tremblay and Yvan Cournoyer—into solid scorers. "The key to everything is my skating," Béliveau once explained. "As a center, I have to be first when we hit the blue line. If I'm a half-step slow, my passes will be intercepted or the wingers will be thrown offside." Even after he retired as a player in 1971, Béliveau continued to lead the Canadiens to victory as a team executive. He

Five Cups in a Row

BETWEEN 1949 AND 1953, THE NEW YORK Yankees won five World Series in a row. The Canadiens saw this as a challenge, and, starting with the 1956 playoffs, they began their own run of five consecutive championships under new coach Toe Blake. With a core of eight future Hall-of-Famers, the Canadiens didn't finish first in the league during the regular season every year, but in the playoffs, they were unstoppable. Only in 1958, the third year of their run, did their opponent in the Cup Finals win more than one game. The team's stars seemed to take turns playing the hero in the postseason. In 1956, Jean Béliveau scored seven times in five games to lead Montreal past the Detroit Red Wings. In Game 1 of the 1957 Finals, Rocket Richard got the Habs off to a great start by scoring four times against the Boston Bruins. Richard was a standout again in 1958 against the Bruins, but he was held scoreless in the 1959 Finals against the Toronto Maple Leafs. So forwards Dickie Moore and Marcel Bonin provided the offensive firepower that time. Jacques Plante starred in 1960, allowing the Maple Leafs just five goals in a four-game sweep.

would be part of 17 Stanley Cup-winning teams in Montreal—10 as a player and 7 as an executive.

In June 1971, the day after Béliveau announced his retirement, the Canadiens drafted their next superstar, a flashy right wing named Guy Lafleur. Montreal general manager Sam Pollock pulled off a series of complicated deals to be able to obtain the young sharpshooter from Thurso, Quebec, who had tallied an astounding 130 goals and added 79 assists in just 62 games in his final year of junior hockey. Pollock was thrilled on draft day, and Lafleur was just as excited to be coming to Montreal. "When I was a kid, all we saw on TV was the Canadiens, and all I wanted to be was Béliveau. We had one *bleu, blanc, et rouge* [blue, white, and red] Canadiens sweater, and I fought the others for the right to wear it. I dreaded to be drafted by any other team but the Canadiens, and when they took me I was so happy." Béliveau offered to

CANADIENS ALL-TIME TEAM

Steve Shutt WING

Perhaps no Canadiens player ever had the work ethic of Steve Shutt. While he was a solid offensive performer, tallying 30-plus goals in 9 consecutive years, Shutt prided himself even more on his all-around game, especially in the postseason. "In the playoffs," he noted, "it was the people I like to call the plumbers—the ones that did all the dirty work—who carried the club. They never get much recognition, but they're the backbone of the team." While Shutt did not receive the same acclaim as his line-mate Guy Lafleur, he was an integral part of five Stanley Cup winners during his years in Montreal.

CANADIENS SEASONS: 1972–85
HEIGHT: 5-11 (180 cm)
WEIGHT: 180 (82 kg)

- 424 career goals
- First NHL left wing to score 60 goals in a season (1976–77)
- 3-time All-Star
- Hockey Hall of Fame inductee (1993)

Canadiens fans nicknamed Guy Lafleur "The Blond Demon" on account of his long hair, wild rushes across the ice, and high-velocity slap shot.

let the rookie wear his number 4 jersey, but Lafleur turned down the honor because he felt fans might expect too much of him right away, choosing number 10 instead.

"It's nice to have fans all over Canada as we did. You don't realize it when you play, but when you're retired and people are talking about the past, it's amazing how many fans know everything about you, even kids who are only 10 or 11 years old."

MONTREAL WING GUY LAFLEUR

In French, Lafleur means "the flower," and the new star helped launch an era in Montreal known as "Flower Power." The new era didn't begin right away, however, as Lafleur struggled his first few years with the Habs. Then, during the 1974–75 season, his fourth in the league, Lafleur decided to take off his helmet and let his blond hair blow freely as he raced up and down the ice. The new look seemed to inspire his play as well, and he scored more than 100 points in a season for the first time.

The next season, Lafleur won his first NHL scoring title and led the Habs to another Stanley Cup. Over the next three years, Lafleur earned two more scoring titles, and the Canadiens, led by stern coach Scotty Bowman, claimed all three Cup championships. Many Montreal fans believe that the Flower Power squad—which featured a first line of Lafleur, huge center Peter Mahovlich, and hard-as-nails winger Steve Shutt; defensive forward supreme Bob Gainey;

A Perfect Penalty

DURING THE 1970S, THE CANADIENS expected to win the Stanley Cup each year. And, in fact, they did win six Cups during the decade. But very few fans expected the Habs to even reach the Finals in 1979. With less than two minutes to go in Game 7 of the Wales Conference Finals against the Boston Bruins, Montreal trailed 4–3. The club's championship run seemed about to end. "Everyone was shaking their heads on the bench because they knew we didn't have much time left," said Montreal winger Guy Lafleur. "The only thing that could save us was a penalty."

And that was just what happened. The Bruins made a disastrous mistake on a line change, and seven Boston players were on the ice at the same time, resulting in a penalty and a Montreal power play. Lafleur and center Jacques Lemaire raced onto the ice, determined to tie the game. Seconds later, Lemaire gained control of the puck in the Boston zone and dropped it back to Lafleur, who sent it sailing into the net. Given new life, the Canadiens defeated the Bruins in overtime and then raced past the New York Rangers in the Stanley Cup Finals in five games.

defensemen Serge Savard, Guy Lapointe, and Larry Robinson; and acrobatic goalie Ken Dryden—was the best Canadiens squad of all time. Don Cherry, who coached the Boston Bruins during those years, marveled at Montreal's powerful roster. "The 1975–76 and 1976–77 Canadiens teams may have been the best ever in the NHL," Cherry later said. "They were even better than the 1980s [Edmonton] Oilers because of the defense."

"Scotty Bowman really pushed players to be better than they ever thought they would be.... Our practices were probably a lot harder than some of the games we played."

MONTREAL WING STEVE SHUTT

CANADIENS ALL-TIME TEAM

Doug Harvey DEFENSEMAN

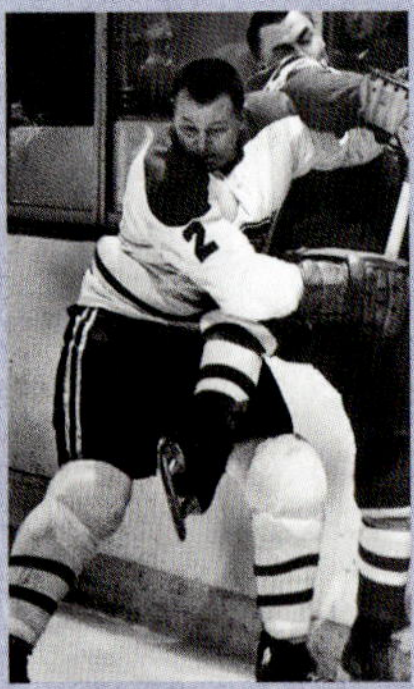

Doug Harvey was a complete player. During the 1950s, when the Canadiens dominated the NHL, Harvey quarterbacked the club's power play, controlled the pace of the game, played hard-nosed defense, blocked shots, and intimidated opponents whenever he joined the action. "Doug Harvey was the best defenseman I ever saw," said former NHL referee Red Storey. "If Montreal got a goal up on you, and Harvey decided you weren't going to score, that was it. Go take a shower, the game was over." Although not a great scorer himself, Harvey's amazing skill as a passer helped him set up goal after goal for his teammates.

CANADIENS SEASONS: 1947–61
HEIGHT: 5-11 (180 cm)
WEIGHT: 190 (86 kg)

- 452 career assists
- 7-time Norris Trophy winner (as best defenseman)
- 13-time All-Star
- Hockey Hall of Fame inductee (1973)

Although not a particularly great shooter, Bob Gainey made up for it with his relentless body checking and stifling defense against opposing stars.

A KING IN GOAL

THE 1980S WERE DOMINATED BY THE New York Islanders and Edmonton Oilers, who won a combined eight Cups. Still, the Canadiens maintained a high level of play throughout the decade, winning five Adams Division titles (as part of the Wales Conference) and reaching the Stanley Cup Finals twice. Several 1970s stars, including Gainey and Robinson, were still around to lead the team and were joined by center Bobby Smith and winger Mats Naslund, the club's first-ever Swedish star. Then, before the 1985–86 season, the Canadiens brought up a 20-year-old rookie goalie named Patrick Roy.

Always calm under pressure, Patrick Roy won the Conn Smythe Trophy as playoffs Most Valuable Player three times in his illustrious career.

Roy, whose name comes from the French word for "king," was solid but unspectacular during his first regular season, but he was majestic in the 1986 playoffs. He was in goal for all 20 Montreal contests, won 15 of them, and allowed opponents fewer than two goals per game. Canadiens fans and teammates still remember Roy's spectacular save in the closing seconds of Game 5 of the Cup Finals against the Calgary Flames that sealed the team's world-championship-clinching victory. "For a rookie to come up that big in the playoffs was amazing," said Montreal center Bobby Smith. "All these years later, I don't know how you could pick anybody else as the best goalie of all time." Roy was awarded the Conn Smythe Trophy as the MVP of the playoffs, the youngest player ever to win the award.

Roy was even more impressive the next time the Canadiens won the Cup, in 1993. He was in the nets for all 16 Montreal victories that postseason, including

CANADIENS ALL-TIME TEAM

Jacques Laperriere DEFENSEMAN

Jacques Laperriere arrived in Montreal the year after his idol, Doug Harvey, retired and took over Harvey's position and his number 2 sweater. During a 12-season career in Montreal that included 6 Stanley Cup triumphs, Laperriere filled Harvey's shoes well while establishing his own defensive style on the ice. With his tall frame and long arms, Laperriere developed an uncanny ability to break up opponents' plays and then quickly move the puck up the ice to set up scoring chances for his teammates. After his playing days, Laperriere remained an important part of the Canadiens' organization, serving as an assistant coach for 16 seasons.

CANADIENS SEASONS: 1962–74
HEIGHT: 6-2 (188 cm)
WEIGHT: 190 (86 kg)

- 242 career assists
- 5-time All-Star
- 1966 Norris Trophy winner
- Hockey Hall of Fame inductee (1987)

Big defenseman Larry Robinson enjoyed more than his share of playoff success, playing in the postseason every year for 20 straight seasons.

10 sudden-death overtime wins. "We didn't mind going into overtime," said Roy. "I knew my teammates were going to score goals if I gave them time."

Unfortunately, following the 1993 Cup triumph, Montreal's fortunes began to turn. Roy suffered an appendicitis attack in the first round of the 1994 playoffs, and the Canadiens were quickly eliminated by the Boston Bruins. The following season, the club failed to make the playoffs for the first time in 25 years. Much of the blame was placed on Roy, and he began to feud with team management. When he was left in the nets in a December 1995 blowout in which he gave up an embarrassing total of nine goals, Roy demanded to be traded. Four days later, he was sent to the Colorado Avalanche.

Many Montreal fans came to believe that losing Roy in "Le Trade" put a curse on their team. Roy led the Avalanche to Stanley Cups in 1996 and 2001 and retired in 2003 as the NHL's all-time leading goalie in regular-season and playoff victories. Meanwhile, the Canadiens seemed to lose their winning touch without Roy's special magic in goal.

Working Overtime

POSTSEASON HOCKEY GAMES INVOLVE 60 minutes of play. But if they end in a tie, the contest heads into sudden-death overtime, with the first team to score being declared the winner. The Canadiens and their star goalie, Patrick Roy, were involved in a whopping 11 sudden-death situations during the 1993 postseason and won 10 of those overtime contests on their way to earning their 24th Stanley Cup. The postseason ended well but started poorly, as the Canadiens lost Game 1 in the first round to the Quebec Nordiques in overtime. Then they won two overtime games themselves and soon captured the series. In round two, the Canadiens swept the Buffalo Sabres in four straight games, but the last three wins required an extra session. Roy came up big in two more sudden-death situations in the next round against the New York Islanders and three in the Cup Finals against the Los Angeles Kings. "The King" ruled in these 10 extra periods, facing 65 shots and turning away every one. In all, he allowed just one goal in 216 minutes of overtime play. "My concentration was at such a high level," Roy told reporters. "My mind was right there. I felt fresh, like I could stop everything."

CANADIENS

The Canadiens missed the playoffs for three straight years before goalie José Théodore and his teammates fought to the postseason in 2002.

CANADIENS

NEW HOME, NEW FACES

ROY'S DEPARTURE WAS JUST THE BEGINNING of an era of change in Montreal. In March 1996, the Habs moved into a new home, the Molson Centre (renamed the Bell Centre in September 2002), and began a slow rebuilding process. Montreal fans, accustomed to cheering for a contender, grew impatient when the club failed to make the playoffs in 1999, 2000, and 2001.

By the 2001–02 season, the Canadiens were led by a new coach, Michel Therrien, and a new star, goaltender José Théodore. Théodore carried the Habs back to the playoffs in 2002 by leading all NHL goalies during the regular season with a sensational .931 save percentage. For his efforts, he was awarded both the Vezina Trophy and the Hart Trophy,

Michel Therrien took his first NHL head coaching job in Montreal in 2001–02 and directed the Canadiens to an upset win in the 2002 playoffs.

becoming the first Montreal player to be named league MVP since Guy Lafleur in 1978. "Lafleur was one of my idols," said Théodore. "I'm very happy to be a Montreal Canadien right now."

Théodore got some unexpected support in the 2002 playoffs when Finnish center and team captain Saku Koivu returned to the ice after missing nearly the entire season while being treated for cancer. Inspired by Koivu's courage and play, the Habs defeated the Eastern Conference's top seed, the Boston Bruins, in the first round of the playoffs. Then they nearly upset the Carolina Hurricanes in the second round before succumbing in six games.

Théodore arrived in training camp the next season out of shape, setting a poor tone for the rest of the club. The Habs recorded their fourth losing campaign in five years, missing the playoffs once again. Following the season, former Canadiens captain Bob Gainey took over as general manager and

CANADIENS ALL-TIME TEAM

Jacques Plante GOALIE

Before Jacques Plante came along, most goalies stayed near the net and waited for opposing players to fire shots at them. Plante changed that. He moved around, often leaving the goal crease to intercept opponents and cut down their angle on a shot. One reporter wrote, "Plante plays in front of the net, beside it, behind it. Some night, he'll probably be found on top of it." Plante was a standout during the Canadiens' string of five consecutive Stanley Cups (1956–60) and won the Vezina Trophy each of those years. He also made hockey history in 1959, becoming the first goaltender to wear a mask during games.

CANADIENS SEASONS: 1952–63
HEIGHT: 6-0 (183 cm)
WEIGHT: 175 (79 kg)

- 437 career wins
- 82 career shutouts
- 7-time Vezina Trophy winner (as best goaltender)
- Hockey Hall of Fame inductee (1978)

José Théodore was drafted by Montreal in 1994 but found little success in the late 1990s before breaking through as a star in 2001–02.

promised to improve the organization. He strengthened the team up front by signing rookie winger Michael Ryder and trading for winger Alexei Kovalev, and the two newcomers joined Koivu and center Mike Ribeiro in spearheading the Habs' offensive attack. The 2003–04 Canadiens put on a late-season charge to finish with 41 wins and earn a postseason berth. Then they surprised the Bruins again, storming back from a three-games-to-one deficit in the first round to triumph in seven games. However, they were no match for the eventual Cup champion Tampa Bay Lightning in the next round, losing four straight contests. "We had a great run, but it's frustrating," said Théodore. "But this is a building process for the future."

"As a goalie, you don't look at the number of goals, you just make sure there are no weak ones."

MONTREAL GOALTENDER JOSÉ THÉODORE

The future would be delayed for a year, however, when the 2004–05 season was cancelled because of a player lockout by league owners in a dispute over the establishment of a players' salary cap. In 2005–06, with the spat finally resolved, the Habs got off to a fast 12–4 start and looked like the surprise of the league. Then they came back to Earth and declined even more when Théodore was forced to sit out with a heel injury. His replacement, French goalie Cristobal Huet, performed so well that the Canadiens decided to trade Théodore to Colorado for Swiss goalie David Aebischer. The team's

Named team captain in 1999, fan favorite Saku Koivu remained a top player even after a bout with cancer in 2001 and a serious eye injury in 2006.

new goaltending duo provided a spark that helped the Canadiens reach the playoffs for the 77th time in their history. But the seventh-seeded Habs were quickly eliminated in the opening round by the Carolina Hurricanes, the eventual Stanley Cup champs that year.

The Canadiens finished with a winning record in 2006–07 as well (42–34–6) but came up one victory shy of qualifying for the postseason. Still, two straight winning campaigns, a strong start to 2007–08, and the presence of young stars such as Ryder and strapping defenseman Sheldon Souray gave Montreal fans hope for a return to glory.

The Canadiens have come a long way since their early days skating on a frigid outdoor rink. Over the years, "Les Habitants" have united both French- and English-speaking Canadians who take pride in rooting for hockey's most successful club. Today's collection of Canadiens plans to reestablish that winning tradition in Montreal and add world championship number 25 to the franchise's trophy case.

"It wasn't just winning that mattered in Montreal; you needed to win with passion and grace, lifting people out of their seats."

SPORTSWRITER ERIC DUHATSCHEK

Centennial Symbols

TO CELEBRATE THEIR 100TH ANNIVERSARY in 2009, the Canadiens will unveil a special centennial logo. The new logo incorporates many of the team's traditional symbols, plus a fanciful "100" printed in the team's colors of *bleu, blanc, et rouge* (blue, white, and red). Symbolism has always played an important role in the history of the Canadiens. The team's colors, for example, are the colors of the flag of France and are symbolic of Montreal's French heritage. The letters in the team's logo—a large H surrounded by a C—also have a special meaning. The H doesn't stand for "Habs," as some people mistakenly think, but for "hockey," since the team's official name is "Le Club de Hockey Canadien." The club's earliest logo had an A inside the C instead of an H because it was originally named "Le Club Athletique Canadien." The team's red home jersey is another treasured symbol for hockey fans, who call it *La Sainte-Flanelle* ("the holy sweater"). While most Canadiens symbols have a long tradition, the team's mascot—a furry, orange creature named "Youppi"—didn't come on board until 2004. He was inherited from the Montreal Expos baseball club after that franchise moved south to become the Washington Nationals.

Hector "Toe" Blake COACH

Before becoming a coaching legend, Hector "Toe" Blake was an All-Star left wing with the Canadiens, earning two Stanley Cup rings, a league MVP award, and a Lady Byng Trophy for sportsmanship. He was even more successful as a coach. In his 13 years at the helm, Blake's Canadiens teams never posted a losing record or failed to make the playoffs. They captured the Stanley Cup in each of Blake's first five seasons behind the bench and won eight Cups total during his coaching career. "I felt that if we didn't finish first, I wouldn't have done a good job," Blake once said.

CANADIENS SEASONS AS COACH: 1955–68
NHL COACHING RECORD: 500–255–159
STANLEY CUP CHAMPIONSHIPS WITH MONTREAL: 1956, 1957, 1958, 1959, 1960, 1965, 1966, 1968
HOCKEY HALL OF FAME INDUCTEE (1966)

CANADIENS

CANADIENS

The bilingual Bell Centre, featuring signs in both English and French (as is common throughout Montreal), hosted playoff games in 2002, 2004, and 2006.

CANADIENS

INDEX

CANADIENS